Bertie Bigroar
Finds His Voice

Daisy Meadows

ORCHARD

Scribble
Thicket

Stationery
Station

Toadstool
Cafe

Clever-feather's
nting Shed

Woollyhop Shop

Forest Halt Station

Harmony Hall
Theatre

asure
Tree

Moo-Moo
Milkshake Hut

Garland
Green

Sparklepaw
Cottage

Map of Friendship Forest

Can you keep a secret? I thought you could!

Then I'll tell you about an enchanted wood.

It lies through the door in the old oak tree,

Let's go there now - just follow me!

We'll find adventure that never ends,

And meet the Magic Animal Friends!

Love,
Goldie the Cat

Story One
Eggnapped!

CHAPTER ONE: Goldie's Plan   9

CHAPTER TWO: Lions!   25

CHAPTER THREE: Chameleon Chaos   39

CHAPTER FOUR: True Colours   55

CHAPTER FIVE: A Pearl in the River   63

CHAPTER ONE

Goldie's Plan

Lily Hart and her best friend, Jess Forester, were kneeling on the sunny lawn in Lily's garden.

"Here, girl!" called Lily.

"Here, boy!" said Jess.

They each held out a bone-shaped biscuit. But the two chow-chow puppies

on the lawn were so busy wrestling with
each other that they didn't pay any
attention. Their golden fur fluffed up
all around them like cotton wool, and
their tiny pink tongues stuck out as they
panted.

They had been found wandering the
woods with hurt paws. Someone had
brought them in to the Helping Paw
Wildlife Hospital, which Lily's parents
ran from a barn in their garden. Now
the puppies were better, and in just a few
hours, their owner would be arriving to
pick them up.

Lily held up the biscuits again. "Here, doggies!"

"Maybe if we hide, they'll come and look for us," said Jess.

The girls crept over to a bush and ducked down behind it. Then they both called together: "Here, puppies!"

Sure enough, the puppies stopped barking. Then the girls heard trotting paws, and the pair of little chow-chows dashed around the side of the bush.

"Good dogs!" said Lily, laughing as she gave them each a biscuit.

"Let's try it again," said Jess. "Only this time, we'll hide behind a pen."

The girls backed away, then hid behind a rabbit hutch. "Here, puppies!" they called together.

Paws came padding towards them. Then a furry golden face peeked round the side of the hutch ...

Jess gasped. "Goldie!"

The golden cat purred as she wound

 12

her way between their legs, tail upright
in greeting. Jess and Lily bent to stroke
their friend. Goldie was no ordinary
cat — she came from the magical world
of Friendship Forest, where the animals
could talk and walked on their hind legs.

"You know what this means," said
Lily. "It must be time to go to Friendship
Forest for another adventure."

Goldie purred and dashed off across the
lawn.

"Stay here, puppies!" said Jess, then the
girls ran after Goldie. They knew that no
time would pass at Helping Paw while

13

they were away in Friendship Forest.

They all ran to the stream at the bottom of the garden, which sparkled in the sunshine. Then Goldie hopped over the stepping stones into Brightley Meadow, where a huge, dead old oak tree stood. As the cat came closer, the tree's branches burst into life. Bright green leaves sprouted from every twig, and colourful blossoms swirled around its trunk. A trio of larks settled on the highest branch, twittering merrily to each other.

"The Friendship Tree!" cried Jess and Lily, at the same time.

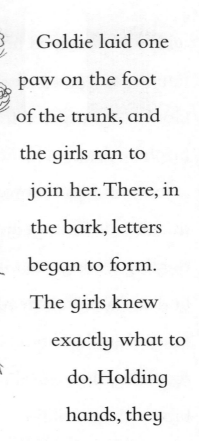

Goldie laid one paw on the foot of the trunk, and the girls ran to join her. There, in the bark, letters began to form. The girls knew exactly what to do. Holding hands, they read the words out loud. "Friendship Forest!"

A little door appeared in the tree trunk,

with a leaf-shaped handle. Lily turned the handle, and Jess pushed the door open. Golden light spilled from inside, even brighter than sunshine.

Jess and Lily followed Goldie through, ducking down together to fit inside. A tingling feeling ran all through their bodies from their heads to their toes. They knew that the magic of the forest was shrinking them until they were not much bigger than Goldie.

Suddenly the golden light vanished, and the girls found themselves standing in a woodland glade. A gentle breeze

blew through the trees, ruffling a carpet
of colourful summer flowers at their
feet. Flowers grew in every colour of the
rainbow! Even the trees had beautiful
flowers winding up their trunks and
dangling from their branches.

"Welcome back to Friendship Forest!"
said Goldie, with a smile. The golden cat
was standing on her hind legs now, and
wore her favourite sparkly scarf.

Jess and Lily ran over and wrapped the
cat up in a big hug. "It's so good to be
here again!" cried Lily.

"And the forest looks even more

beautiful than usual," added Jess. She
pointed up at the clear blue sky. "Look –
not a single cloud!"

"That's because it's Midsummer's
Day," said Goldie. "And just wait ... the
Midsummer Festival is about to begin! It's
so much fun. There are three big events.

First there's the Super

Swim Show,

then there's

the Bake-Off

Bonanza

and the

Sunshine

Fete too. And at the very end of the day there's a big concert!"

"It does sound amazing!" said Lily, laughing.

"But I hope Grizelda doesn't show up to ruin it," said Jess.

Grizelda was a wicked witch, and she was always trying to take over the forest and drive out the animals who lived there.

"Just let her try!" said Goldie. "You see, I think I've found a way to protect Friendship Forest from Grizelda ... for ever!"

The girls exchanged a puzzled glance.

"That would be brilliant," said Lily. "But how?"

Goldie put her paws to her mouth and called out into the forest. "Mr Bigroar! Mrs Bigroar! Meet Lily and Jess!"

The bushes rustled, then two huge golden creatures stepped out into the clearing. Jess and Lily both gasped in shock.

Lions!

Mr Bigroar wore a shiny bowler hat, and Mrs Bigroar had a pair of yellow-framed glasses perched on the end of her snout. She flicked her tail, making the

flowers flutter.

Lily and Jess held hands again, more tightly this time, both feeling a little afraid of the lions.

Two fuzzy little golden cubs tumbled out of the bushes behind the big lions, rolling and scrapping. Then a third, slightly bigger cub pushed through the trees. His fur gleamed, and he wore a blue hat with his fluffy ears poking out of the top.

"Beatrice, Beau, stop that," he said, pulling them apart. "Sorry," he said to the girls and Goldie. "They're only little and they like to play."

"Just like the puppies at home," Lily whispered, feeling less scared.

"Bertie is our eldest," Mr Bigroar said. "He's very good at taking care of his brother and sister."

Bertie pawed the ground shyly. "I do

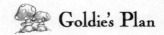

my best," he mumbled.

Jess laughed. "Well,
you certainly sound
like a very helpful
cub."

The little lion puffed
out his chest with pride.

"The Bigroars are
distant relatives of mine," explained
Goldie. "They come from Pleasant Plains,
far beyond the forest. I invited them here
so that they can protect the animals from
Grizelda."

"Great idea, Goldie," said Jess. Grizelda

would be far too afraid to do anything to the forest with a pride of lions running around.

"Welcome to Friendship Forest!" Lily said.

"Oh, thank you!" said Mr Bigroar, with a tip of his hat. "It would be such an honour to help keep the animals here safe… I just hope we're not too scary for them. You're not scared of us, are you?"

Lily and Jess exchanged a look. Then they both smiled and shook their heads. "Maybe at first," said Jess. "But not any more!"

CHAPTER TWO

Lions!

"Come on then," said Goldie, with a smile. "It's not far to the Midsummer Festival. I'm going to introduce you to all the animals in Friendship Forest!"

They set off through the trees, with Goldie leading the way. Soon they arrived at Sunshine Meadow, a big field

filled with red, orange and yellow flowers.
But today it was full of animals too,
chattering and laughing in the sun. They
crowded around little stalls and stages
set up all over the meadow. Jaunty music
filled the girls' ears. Colourful banners
fluttered in a gentle breeze, and delicious
food smells wafted towards them.

"The Midsummer Festival!" squealed
Bertie.

"That's right," said Goldie. "Follow me."

Goldie led them towards the crowd
of happy animals. The girls saw a little
group of squirrels hopping excitedly

beside a face-painting stall, each getting a sparkly butterfly painted on their faces by a smiling old hedgehog. They spotted a coconut shy and cheered when Rusty Fuzzybrush the fox cub knocked off the biggest coconut and won a fluffy teddy bear twice as big as he was.

"Blossom buns!" said Lily, pointing to a table loaded with the pale pink and yellow treats.

"Yum!" said Jess. "I can't wait to enjoy the festival!"

Goldie was busy speaking to Mr Silverback the badger. Mr Silverback

handed over
a red shiny
megaphone,
then Goldie
beckoned the

girls over and climbed up on to a little

stage. "This is a magic megaphone," she

explained. "When you speak through

it, your voice carries to every corner of

Friendship Forest!"

Goldie pressed a button on the handle

of the megaphone and spoke. "Hello,

everyone!" she said. Her voice crackled

out across the meadow. All the animals

stopped what they were doing and turned

round to look. "I'd like to introduce you

to some relatives of mine. I hope you'll all

welcome … the Bigroars!"

Goldie pointed to where the lion family

stood close to the stage. At once a hush

fell. Then Mr Gigglepip the guinea pig

pointed a trembling

paw at them.

"Lions!" he

squeaked. "Run!"

The animals ran,

ducking under awnings,

diving behind tents and

Lions!

scrambling under rugs.

Mr Bigroar's mane drooped, and Mrs Bigroar held her cubs close.

"Oh dear," mumbled Bertie. "Maybe this wasn't such a good idea."

"It's all right, everyone," Jess called through the megaphone. "There's no need to be afraid!"

"They're nice lions," added Lily. "We promise! Goldie's brought them here to protect the forest from Grizelda."

There was a pause. Then finally, here and there, a few furry little heads poked up out of hiding places. A duckling

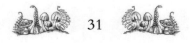

clambered out of a big apple crate and waddled towards them. She had wellies on, and a crown made of daisies. "That's Ellie Featherbill," Jess whispered to the lion family.

"Have you really come to protect us?" asked Ellie, nervously.

Bertie scampered out from between his mother's legs and gave a little bow. Then he held out a fuzzy paw. "We promise!" he said.

Ellie threw her fluffy wings around him. "Hurrah!" she squealed.

All the other animals bounded out of

their hiding places and clustered around the lions, hugging them and shaking Mr and Mrs Bigroar by the paw.

Lily and Jess gave their duckling friend a big hug too.

"Oh, it's so good to see you girls again!" said Ellie. "Will you come and visit my family on the barge? Mum laid an egg and it's going to hatch any moment now."

"Can I come too?" asked Bertie, shyly.

"I've never seen an egg hatch before."

"Of course you can!" said Ellie.

"So long as your parents don't mind," added Goldie, handing the megaphone back to Mr Silverback.

Mr Bigroar shook his big head. "You go and enjoy yourself, Bertie," he said. "We'll stay here and get to know everyone." He bent down low, so that the giggling Twinkletail family of mice could nuzzle up to his mane.

Ellie skipped ahead, and the girls, Goldie and Bertie followed her over the meadow and down to Willowtree River.

There the Featherbill barge was moored, its coat of pale blue paint gleaming in the sunshine. On the front deck the family of ducks all clustered around a little green cot.

The girls, Ellie, Goldie and Bertie climbed aboard, and peered into the cot. A smooth, pale-blue egg sat inside, speckled with brown.

"It's so pretty!" whispered Bertie, his big dark eyes open wide.

"You must be one of the Bigroars!" said Mr Featherbill. "Welcome to—"

But before he could finish, the egg in

 35

the cot wobbled.

"I think it's hatching!" said Jess.

Sure enough, the egg shook again. The friends all held hands in excitement.

"Here comes the baby!" said Mrs Featherbill, beaming.

 36

Crack! A fine dark line spread across the surface of the egg.

FIZZZZ! Jess and Lily dodged as a bright green spark shot out and fizzled on the deck.

"Is that normal?" asked Bertie.

"Not at all!" said Mr Featherbill.

"What's happening?" said Mrs Featherbill anxiously, as her ducklings all scurried to hide behind her.

CRACK! The top of the egg flew off, and something leapt out from inside, landing on all fours on the deck. It was a tiny green lizard with a long tail. It

shimmered with
a strange green
glow.

"That's not a
duck!" said Lily.

"It looks like

... a lizard," said Jess.

"It's a chameleon!" said Goldie. "What's
it doing here?"

CHAPTER THREE

Chameleon Chaos

The baby lizard flicked its tail, then stamped its feet crossly, one by one. It made a funny, angry little gurgling sound. Then without warning it set off, racing around the deck at top speed. The Featherbills all squawked in alarm, and even Bertie the lion cub shrank back and

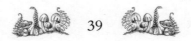

curled up his tail.

As it ran, the lizard went *POP!* It
turned into a little duckling.

"Huh?" gasped Ellie Featherbill. "Now
it looks just like my brother Rodney!"

POP! The lizard changed again,
turning into a cat with a sparkly scarf.

"And now it looks like me!" said
Goldie.

POP!

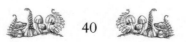

"What's going on?!" said Lily, turning to Jess.

But with a *POP*, Jess transformed into the lizard! Lily gasped. She whirled around – and was relieved to see the real Jess standing behind her.

"I thought it was you!" Lily said. "It looked exactly like you."

"It's a chameleon," said Goldie, "and it's magically changing shape!"

"But if that was a chameleon egg," said Mr Featherbill, pointing at the broken blue shell, "where is *our* egg?"

"I think I might know," said Goldie. She

pointed upstream.

There, hovering in the air, was a
yellowish-green orb of light. It came
floating towards them like a nasty bubble
of swamp water.

"Oh no," gasped Lily. "Grizelda!"

The orb exploded in a sudden shower
of green sparks, and a figure landed on
the front of the barge. It was Grizelda,
wearing a shiny purple dress. She had a
horrid scowl and long, crinkly green hair.

"Friendship Forest will soon be mine!"
Grizelda boasted. "I've come up with
my cleverest plan yet ... I've swapped

three forest eggs

with three

chameleon eggs!

And I've cast

a particularly

nasty spell on

the eggs too, so

that my baby

chameleons will

ruin the forest! These pesky animals will

have to leave, and the whole place will be

mine at last!" She threw back her head

and laughed horribly. "You won't stop me

this time! Chameleon, do your worst!"

At Grizelda's words, the little chameleon let out a grumpy squawk then dived off the side of the barge. The girls saw it splashing its way to the bank. Then it shot off and disappeared among the trees.

"What have you done with the real eggs?" Lily demanded.

Grizelda tapped her nose. "You'll never find them!"

Bertie Bigroar stepped forward bravely. "Leave her to me!" he said. Then he frowned sternly at Grizelda, took a deep breath and opened his jaws …

"Meow!" Bertie
squeaked. He sounded
just like a kitten.

"Is that
supposed to be
scary?" sneered
Grizelda. "Silly
lion can't even
roar properly!"

BANG! Green smoke billowed up from
the deck. And when it cleared, Grizelda
had completely vanished.

"Our egg," wailed Mrs Featherbill,
flapping her wings. "She's taken it!" All

 45

the other Featherbills crowded round, wrapping her up in a big hug.

"We'll get it back, dear," said Mr Featherbill. "Somehow …"

"It's my fault," said Bertie Bigroar. His tail had drooped, and he hung his head sadly. "I'm supposed to be protecting the forest, and I couldn't even scare off that mean witch! If only I could do a proper roar, like Mum and Dad …"

"Don't be so hard on yourself," said Jess, stroking Bertie's soft fur. "She went away, didn't she?"

"And besides, we can still get that egg

46

back," added Lily.

"We just have to find it," agreed Goldie.

"Do you really think you can do it?" asked little Ellie Featherbill.

Lily and Jess looked at each other and nodded. "We promise," they said together.

"I'll come too!" said Bertie. "Which way do we go?"

Before the girls could answer, they heard a commotion from further down the river – a big splash, and a chorus of anxious animal voices.

"Sounds like trouble," said Goldie. "Let's see what's going on."

"We'll be back soon!" Lily promised the Featherbills. Then she and Jess raced over the gangplank with Goldie and Bertie. They hurried along the bank, heading round a bend in the river to see where the noise had come from.

There was a crowd of animals on the bank, where three wooden diving boards had been set up. But one of them had toppled into the river, and Violet Flippershell the turtle was floundering around in the water beside it. Her friends were leaning over the bank, desperately trying to reach her.

"Oh dear!" said Goldie. "She must have been practising for the Swim Show. It's supposed to start soon."

"Look!" cried Lily. She pointed to the bank, where little Frankie Greenhop the frog was hopping up and down and furiously stamping her feet, right beside where the diving board had stood.

"You don't think Frankie pushed the board

over, do you?" said Jess, frowning. "She's

such a nice frog!"

Frankie shoved her way through the

crowd to a pile of rubber rings. One by

one she grabbed them

and stomped on them.

BANG! BANG!

BANG! The animals

all covered their ears

at the sounds of the

rings bursting.

"What's got into

her?" wondered Lily.

Just then, a little green figure came

running along the bank. "I'm sorry I'm late," panted Frankie Greenhop. "I was having too much fun at the fete and I lost track of time!"

Jess and Lily stared in astonishment at her, then back at the frog stomping on the rubber rings.

"One of them must be the chameleon," said Jess. "And I bet I know which …"

Lily ran towards the frog by the rubber rings. "You stop that right now!"

The frog scowled. Then all of a sudden – *POP!* – she transformed into Ellie Featherbill!

"I knew it!" said Jess.

"I'll catch him!" cried Bertie.

The little lion pounced at the chameleon-duckling, but she darted away, disappearing in among the crowd of animals on the bank. Jess, Lily and Goldie ran after her, peering over the heads of the crowd. But there was no sign of the chameleon-duckling anywhere.

SPLASH! Chloe Slipperslide the otter went tumbling into the river. A moment later the otter's head popped up. She looked puzzled. "Someone pushed me!" she cried.

"There!" called Jess, pointing at Mr Flippershell, who was stomping and shoving his way through the crowd. "That must be that naughty chameleon, in disguise again."

"I don't like this," said Goldie. "Sooner or later he's going to cause a bad accident. We'd better catch him right away."

"But how can we catch him if he keeps changing what he looks like?" asked Lily. "It must be that spell Grizelda put on him. We need to break it somehow."

The girls thought for a moment.

"We aren't far from the Muddlepups'
garden. Maybe they will know a potion
or spell that could help?" said Jess. The
Muddlepups were a family of golden
Labradors who had a garden full of
magical plants.

"Great idea!" said Lily.

And the friends ran as fast as they
could. If they didn't stop the chameleon
soon, who knew what damage he'd
cause?

CHAPTER FOUR
True Colours

Poppy and Patch Muddlepup were in the garden, watering their magical plants. As soon as the twin puppies saw the girls, they put down their watering cans and bounded over to say hello.

"What pretty flowers!" said Bertie, as he came puffing to a halt beside Goldie.

"You must be Bertie," said Poppy shyly. "Hello!"

"We're trying to water the flowers as fast as we can," explained Patch, "so we can go to the Midsummer Festival!"

Quickly the girls explained about the chameleon, and how it kept turning into different animals.

Poppy scratched her ear thoughtfully. "It sounds like you need a True Colours Potion. That should stop it transforming!"

"Perfect," said Goldie. "But how do we make it?"

"First we have to collect a petal in

every colour of the rainbow," said Patch.

The friends got to work, hunting through the garden. Soon they had got seven different coloured petals – red, orange, yellow, green, blue, indigo and violet.

Then Poppy picked up a bowl full of crystal-clear rainwater. She dropped the petals in one by one, and stirred them with a paw.

The potion began to shimmer as the

petals dissolved, swirling into a rainbow-coloured whirlpool.

"It's beautiful!" gasped Bertie, his whiskers quivering. "I've never seen magic like this before!"

Patch dived into the cottage and came back a moment later with a little glass spray bottle. The puppies poured the colourful liquid in and handed it to Goldie.

"All you need to do is squirt the chameleon with the potion," said Poppy. "Then you'll see him as he really is!"

"Thank you!" said Jess and Lily.

"Let's hurry!" said Goldie.

They raced back through the forest as fast as they could.

The riverbank was still crowded with animals when they arrived, but this time it was easy to see where the chameleon was. Mr Flippershell bobbed in the river, muttering angrily to himself and splashing water at everyone on the bank.

"I don't want to get wet!" squealed a little squirrel. But Mr Flippershell splashed her anyway.

"That's got to be the chameleon," said Jess. "The real Mr Flippershell would

never be so mean!"

"Let's spray him with the potion!" said Bertie.

Lily took the bottle from Goldie, then she and Jess crept along the river bank until they were very close to Mr Flippershell.

"Now!" cried Jess, and Lily sprayed the bottle.

Hssss! A fine rainbow mist settled on Mr Flippershell. For an instant the turtle flickered, and the girls saw the chameleon beneath the disguise, surrounded by the strange green glow they'd noticed when

he first hatched. Then he turned straight
back into a turtle.

"Try it again," said Goldie. But the
second time, the chameleon turned back
into a turtle even faster.

"The potion's not working!" said Lily.
"Oh dear ... Grizelda's spell must be too
strong for the Muddlepups' magic."

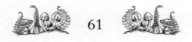

Mr Flippershell glared at the girls and stuck his tongue out.

"He's very cross, isn't he?" whispered Jess.

"He's the grumpiest baby we've ever met!" agreed Lily.

"Do you think we could make him happy instead?" said Bertie thoughtfully. "Then maybe he'd stop all this mischief!"

"It's worth a try," said Jess. "But how do we make a baby chameleon happy ... ?"

CHAPTER FIVE

A Pearl in the River

"I know!" said Bertie. "When my brother and sister were newborns, I always used to tickle them to make them laugh. Maybe if we tickle the chameleon, we can cheer him up!"

"That might work," said Goldie, "if we could only reach him somehow …"

The girls looked all around. Then Lily
darted over to some long reeds and picked
two of them. She handed one to Jess. They
both leaned out as far as they dared over
the river, reaching towards the chameleon
with their reeds …

"Tickle tickle!" said Jess, wiggling the
reed so it brushed under Mr Flippershell's
chin.

Mr Flippershell squawked and bobbed
away.

"Tickle tickle!" said Lily, brushing her
reed against the turtle's flippers.

"Tee hee hee!" laughed Mr Flippershell.

He tried to scowl, but his lips were curving into a smile.

As the girls kept tickling, Mr Flippershell kept wriggling, and the river current carried him gently to the bank. Goldie and Bertie bent down and scooped him out. Bertie gave the turtle another little tickle, then Mr Flippershell made a happy, gurgling sound, and all

at once – *POP!* – he turned back into
the baby chameleon. Bertie cradled the
chameleon gently in his silky paws and
wrapped him up in a big, soft hug.

"Bertie's good with babies, isn't he?"
whispered Jess.

"Must be because he
helps look after his
little brother and
sister," said Lily.
The chameleon's
strange green glow
faded and he smiled
and snuggled up to

Bertie's warm chest. Within moments, he was fast asleep.

"That must mean we've broken the spell!" said Goldie. "But we still have to find the Featherbills' missing egg …"

SPLOOSH! The girls turned to see Violet Flippershell come shooting out of the water and bob on the surface. "Look what I've found, everyone!" cried Violet, holding something smooth and blue in her front flippers. "I think it's an enormous blue pearl! But it's a funny shape …"

Jess gasped. "That's not a pearl … That's the missing egg!"

"Mean old Grizelda must have hidden it in the river," said Lily. "Well done, Violet! We'll take it back to the Featherbills right away."

The girls wrapped the egg in Goldie's scarf to keep it warm. Then they hurried back to the Featherbills' barge, with Goldie close behind and Bertie still carrying the snoozing chameleon. The Featherbill family were all clustered on the front deck. But when they saw Jess and Lily gently lay the egg down in its cot, they all started quacking and flapping their wings with joy.

Crrrraack! A fine dark line spread across the surface of the egg.

"It's hatching!" whispered Goldie.

"I just hope this one isn't a chameleon …" muttered Jess.

With another crack, the egg broke clean in two. Inside, the tiniest, fluffiest duckling sat blinking up at them. It was bright yellow, with an orange beak and little black eyes like wet pebbles.

"It's so cute!" cried Lily.

Mr and Mrs Featherbill scooped up the tiny duckling in a blanket and cuddled it between them. "What shall we call her?"

asked Mrs Featherbill.

"How about Pearl?" Bertie piped up.
"That's what Violet thought she was at
first."

"What a pretty name!" said Mr
Featherbill. "Pearl Featherbill, welcome to
Friendship Forest!"

Pearl gave a little quack, and her

brothers and sisters all cheered.

Suddenly, in the distance, a brass band began to play a cheerful tune.

"Ooh!" cried Goldie. "That means the first part of the Midsummer Festival is about to begin … the Swim Show!"

"Perfect!" said Mrs Featherbill. "We can introduce Pearl to all the other animals of Friendship Forest!"

Before long the girls were sitting on blankets on the riverbank alongside their friends, watching and clapping as the Flippershell family performed a water-dance, ducking and diving in time to the

music of the brass band.

"This is incredible!" said Jess. "But we mustn't stay long. Grizelda said she stole three eggs, remember? So there are still two left to find!"

"And two chameleons," added Lily.

"But what will we do with this one?" asked Bertie, gazing at the chameleon that lay fast asleep in his paws.

"I know!" said Goldie. She stood and beckoned to a bird with a long beak and even longer legs. "This is Mrs Kinderbeak," said Goldie, as the stork picked its way towards them. "She helps look after all the babies in the forest!"

"I love little ones!" said Mrs
Kinderbeak, bobbing her head. "And who
do we have here?"

"He's a chameleon," said Bertie. "But
I don't know what his name is. Will you
take care of him for us? Until we can find
his mum and dad."

"It would be a pleasure!" said Mrs
Kinderbeak. She unwound a sling from
among her feathers. Then she swept the
baby up with one wing and settled him
gently inside the sling.

"Thank you, Mrs Kinderbeak," said Jess

and Lily together.

"We did it!" sighed
Bertie, happily flicking
his tail. "We saved
Pearl, and we
cheered up that
poor chameleon too!"

"We certainly did," said
Goldie. "Now all we have
to do is find the other two
eggs!"

Story Two
Cake-tastrophe

CHAPTER ONE: Mrs Kinderbeak's List   77

CHAPTER TWO: Bother at the Bake-Off   85

CHAPTER THREE: A Very Little Lion Cub   91

CHAPTER FOUR: Blue Strawberries   101

CHAPTER FIVE: Three Little Chicks   107

CHAPTER ONE

Mrs Kinderbeak's List

Mrs Kinderbeak's home was a big, bushy cottage perched at the top of a tall tree. She came fluttering down from it, and passed a piece of white paper to Lily and Jess.

"There you are!" said Mrs Kinderbeak. "It's a list of all the families in the forest

who are expecting eggs."

"That's perfect!" said Lily. "Now we can work out whose eggs Grizelda has stolen."

The mean witch Grizelda had taken three eggs from three families in Friendship Forest, and replaced them with enchanted chameleon eggs. Lily and Jess had already got back the first egg, but there were two still left to find ...

"Thank you, Mrs Kinderbeak!" said Jess.

"Good luck!" said Mrs Kinderbeak. "I'd better check on the little one." The stork

spread her wings and flew back up to her cottage, where she was looking after the baby chameleon the girls had rescued.

Lily studied the list. "The next family is the Cluckfeathers."

"They're a family of chickens," said Goldie. "And they live near here."

It didn't take long to get there. Right in the middle of some juicy vegetable patches was a cosy farmhouse with a bright red door. A frantic clucking and squawking came from inside the house. Then the door swung open with a bang and Mr and Mrs Cluckfeather ran out,

their feathers all fluffed up with shock.
The chickens were snowy white with
bright red feet, and they each wore a little
tweed cap perched on their head.

"Mr and Mrs Cluckfeather, are you
OK?" asked Goldie.

"Our lovely eggs!" squawked Mrs
Cluckfeather.

"We had three eggs," Mr Cluckfeather
explained. "And one of them had started
to hatch."

"But then some funny green sparks
appeared," said Mrs Cluckfeather. "And
it wasn't our chick that came out, but a

little green chameleon! He jumped on the other eggs, and as soon as he touched them, they vanished into thin air!"

"The chameleon ran off," Mr Cluckfeather said, "and now we don't know where any of our chicks are!"

"Don't worry," said Bertie. "The Featherbills' egg went missing too, and it turned up safe and sound. I'm sure yours will, too."

"The Featherbills' egg was very close to their barge," said Lily. "Perhaps your eggs are still in your house."

"Good thinking," said Goldie. "Let's all

look for them!"

They went inside the farmhouse, into a warm room with soft straw covering the floor. "That's where the eggs were," said Mrs Cluckfeather sadly.

The girls began hunting through the straw. Then Lily felt something hard under her fingertips. "I've got something!" she cried. She lifted it up for the others to see. It was a smooth egg. But it wasn't a normal egg colour – instead, it was the exact same yellow as the straw.

"That's one of our eggs!" gasped Mrs Cluckfeather. "But it's the wrong colour."

What had happened to it?

CHAPTER TWO

Bother at the Bake-Off

"I think I understand," said Jess. "The chameleon didn't make the eggs vanish after all. He just turned them yellow, so Mr and Mrs Cluckfeather couldn't see them!"

"Let's find the others!" said Goldie.

Quickly the friends all got to work, sorting through the straw.

"I've got another one!" cried Bertie, lifting up a second yellow egg.

But, try as they might, they couldn't find the third egg anywhere.

"Oh dear," said Mrs Cluckfeather, as she cradled the two yellow eggs in her wings. "Where could it be?"

Just then, a rustling noise came through the window.

Everyone rushed outside.

"Look!" screeched Mrs Cluckfeather. A little green, glowing creature was running

through a strawberry patch, flicking its
tail and chomping on the strawberries.

"It's that pesky chameleon!" said Mr
Cluckfeather. "He's going to eat all my
lovely fruit!"

"Not if we catch him first," said Bertie,
and he bounded towards the chameleon.

The girls and Goldie followed, running

as fast as they could. But the chameleon saw them coming. At once he dropped the strawberry he was eating and scampered away, disappearing among the trees.

"After him!" cried Goldie.

The girls, Goldie and Bertie rushed off through the forest, following the twitching tail of the chameleon up ahead. But within moments, he had slipped away.

"Uh-oh!" said Bertie. "How will we find him now?"

Just then, Jess heard shouts and banging noises coming from somewhere nearby. "Let's try that way!" she called.

They changed direction, following the sounds. In no time at all they came stumbling out into Sunshine Meadow again. The meadow was much emptier than before, and the strange noises were coming from a long stone building with a thatched roof.

"That's where the Bake-Off Bonanza is being held!" cried Goldie.

Quickly they dashed in through the big open doors of the building. Inside the hall was big and white with timber beams overhead, and the air smelled of baking, with delicious wafts of chocolate and cinnamon. The floor was crowded with ovens and long tables. In between them animals in aprons scurried to and fro, waving wooden spoons and calling out to each other.

"There he goes!"

"Look out, over there!"

Something was causing chaos here. But what?

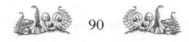

CHAPTER THREE

A Very Little Lion Cub

"It's the chameleon!" shouted Lily.

Sure enough, the little lizard was racing over a tablecloth nearby, scattering scones, cakes and muffins every which way.

"Everything's falling on the floor!"

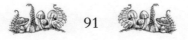

wailed Bertie. "All that hard work is going to waste!"

As the cakes and pastries came to rest on the floor, they flickered, changing colour until they matched the wood they were lying on. "That naughty chameleon," muttered Lily. "He's muddling everything up!"

So many cakes and ingredients had changed colour that all around the hall, the animals were getting confused. Lola Velvetnose held up a pawful of orange powder. "I can't tell if this is brown sugar or white sugar!" she said sadly.

"And my raisins look like redcurrants!" grumbled Woody Flufftail.

"Oh no!" shrieked Mrs Longwhiskers. "I've put ketchup in my blossom buns! I thought it was custard!"

"We have to catch that chameleon right now," said Jess. "Otherwise the whole Bake-Off will be ruined!"

Lily climbed up on a chair to look for

the chameleon. She spotted him at once,
perched on a mountain of cupcakes. He
bit into the one at the very top,
then spat it out again and
scampered off.

"That's strange!"
said Lily. "He
looks hungry,
but he didn't seem
to like that cake."

"He doesn't like any
cake!" added Jess. She
pointed at a lemon cake
with a missing bite, then at

a half-nibbled scone, and a chewed-up pastry. "He keeps spitting things out."

"He must be hungry, so keep trying," said Bertie. "We broke the spell on the last chameleon by making him happy when he was grumpy. Perhaps if we found some food he likes, it might break the spell on this one?"

"Good thinking, Bertie," said Lily. "But what do you think he likes to eat?"

"No time for that," said Goldie. "He's just disappeared!"

The cat pointed to where the chameleon
had been running just a moment before.

Then Jess saw some footprints
appearing in a spilled puddle of flour.
"Over there!" she cried. "After him!"

The friends hurried through the hall,
watching as the footprints streaked
towards the door. They ran outside and
saw the grass swishing as the chameleon
ran back towards the forest.

"We'll never catch him!" sighed Goldie,
as they reached the edge of the trees.

Lily and Jess peered into the forest, but
the little lizard was nowhere to be seen.

Then Lily spotted something. "That leaf has had a bite taken out of it!" she said.

The friends all ran after her to the leaf.

"There!" said Bertie, pointing with his little paw. "Those flowers are missing their petals! The chameleon must have tried to eat them, then spat them out."

"If we keep this up, we might still be able to find him!" said Lily. "Let's go!"

They headed on into the forest, keeping their eyes peeled for more clues.

"I think I just saw something move," said Goldie. "Over there, in those ferns."

As the girls peered closer, the big clump

of ferns rustled, as though something was shuffling around inside it.

"The chameleon must be hiding in there!" whispered Jess.

"Leave it to me!" said Bertie. "Stand back, everyone …"

He tiptoed closer, opened his mouth and …

"Meow!"

Bertie flicked his tail sadly. "I'm sorry, everyone," he mumbled. "I thought maybe I could roar properly when there wasn't a scary witch around."

"Don't worry, Bertie," said Jess, gently

stroking him. "You're still a very little lion cub. One day I'm sure you'll be able to do the biggest roar in the whole forest."

Bertie looked at the ground. "But not in time to save the Cluckfeathers' egg."

CHAPTER FOUR

Blue Strawberries

"I think I've got an idea," said Lily, thoughtfully. "The chameleon ate lots of the Cluckfeathers' strawberries, didn't he? I think he must like those!"

"That's brilliant!" said Jess. "Maybe if we offered him some he'd come out."

"I bet there are some strawberries at

the Bake-Off," said Goldie. "Let's go!"

When they got back to the hall, they found the animals in aprons trying to clear up the terrible mess. There were splodges of multicoloured icing on the walls, cakes all over the floor and even some dollops of sticky purple dough hanging from the ceiling.

Little Beau and Beatrice Bigroar were helping, scooping up sugar with their big paws and stacking cake tins neatly by the ovens. The other animals didn't seem nearly so scared of them any more, and Mrs Longwhiskers even gave Beau a

smile and a cautious pat on the head.

"Excuse me," Jess called out. "Does anyone have any strawberries, please?"

"I do!" piped up Lola Velvetnose the mole. Then her face fell. "Oh, but I haven't a clue where they are! Everything is so messy, and nothing is the right

colour any more. They could be yellow for all I know!"

"Maybe we could sniff them out?" suggested Lily.

They all got to work, following their noses around the hall. But with so many delicious baking smells filling the air, it was hard to pick out strawberries.

"Achoo!" sneezed Jess. "I think I got pepper in my nose."

"I've got something!" cried Lily, holding up a handful of little red things. Then she peered closer. "Oops – actually these are baby carrots, turned red!"

"Look!" called Bertie. He held up a
punnet of berries. Some of them were
yellow and some were blue, but they were
definitely strawberry-
shaped. "Let me taste
one, just to make
sure." Bertie took a
bite and smiled. He
gave the group a big
thumbs-up.

"Well done,
Bertie!" said
Goldie.

In no time at all, they had run back

through the forest and stood panting at the edge of the overgrown patch of ferns.

"Yum, strawberries!" said Lily in a loud voice, so that the chameleon would hear. "I'm just going to leave them here for a moment …"

She put the bowl of multicoloured strawberries down on the grass, then she and Jess, Goldie and Bertie crept off to a big oak tree and hid behind it.

The friends all held their breath, waiting and waiting …

CHAPTER FIVE

Three Little Chicks

Suddenly, the ferns began to rustle and sway.

"I think he's coming!" whispered Bertie, his whiskers quivering with excitement.

Sure enough, a little head popped out. Then the chameleon slithered on to the grass. He was dark green now, exactly the

same colour as the ferns! He still had the
green glow around him.

Jess and Lily watched as the chameleon
took a cautious step forward, sniffing
at the bowl of strawberries. Slowly he
lowered his head and nibbled at a yellow
strawberry. He chewed for a moment.
Then he let out a little squeak of delight
and dived in head first, munching and

chomping his way through the bowl. The green glow around him faded.

"It's working!" said Goldie. "Look!" She pointed at the strawberries, which were turning red again.

Lily grinned. "Everything's going back to its proper colour!"

Bertie crouched on his belly and, ever so gently, he scooped up the chameleon in his big, soft paws. The chameleon was so busy licking strawberry juice off his face that he didn't even seem to notice. He gurgled with happiness.

"Hurrah!" said Lily. "I don't think that

chameleon will be causing any more
trouble."

"Let's return the bowl, then look for the
Cluckfeathers' last egg," said Goldie.

Back at the hall, the animals were
cheerfully baking again, rolling out
dough, mixing ingredients and taking
steaming hot cakes out of ovens.

Only one animal didn't look very
happy.

"Are you all right?" Lily asked Lola
Velvetnose. The little mole was frowning
down at her tray of sticky yellow buns.

Lola picked up one of the buns. "Quite all right, thank you. Except … this bun looks rather strange, don't you think? It's white, for a start."

Jess peered closer and gasped. "Lola, that's not a bun at all! That's an egg!"

"The Cluckfeathers' missing egg!" cried Goldie, clapping her paws. "Oh, well done, Lola – you found it!"

The friends raced back to the
Cluckfeathers' farmhouse. Inside they saw
Mrs Kinderbeak with her wings spread
around Mr and Mrs Cluckfeather.

"There, there," said Mrs Kinderbeak.
"Lily, Jess, Goldie and Bertie will get that
egg back, I'm sure …"

Bertie swung open the door. "We've
already done it!" he cried, proudly. He
carried the snoozing chameleon over
to a little pram that Mrs Kinderbeak
had left by the kitchen table, where the
chameleon from the Swim Show was
already curled up. As Bertie lowered the

second chameleon into the pram, they
both woke and began nuzzling up to each
other, squawking happily.

Jess handed the white egg Lola had
found over to its parents.

"Oh, my feathers!" gasped Mrs Cluckfeather. "How can we ever thank you?"

She and her husband hurried through to the nursery with everyone following. Mr and Mrs Cluckfeather laid the egg down in the straw, nestling it up against their two other eggs, which had turned white again.

Crack! Crack! Crack!

All three eggs broke into little pieces. The girls leaned forward, holding their breath, as three tiny heads poked up from inside. The little chicks were pale

yellow and fluffy, and each one was small
enough to fit in the girls' palms.

"They're adorable!" said Lily, as the
chicks tumbled out of the eggshells.

"They're perfect!" said Mrs
Cluckfeather, as she and her husband
swept the chicks up into a big family
hug. "We've decided to name them Olive,
Peach and Basil – after the things we

grow on our farm."

"Thank you, girls, and Goldie," said Mr Cluckfeather. "You saved our chicks. And thank you, Bertie, too. You're the nicest lion we've ever met!"

Bertie swung his tail and pawed the ground, looking bashful. "You're welcome," he mumbled. Then his stomach gave a big growl. "Oops, that's nearly as loud as a roar! I think I'm almost as hungry as that baby chameleon was."

"And I know just the place we can get something yummy to eat," said Goldie with a smile. "To the Bake-Off!"

Story Three
The Sunshine Fete

CHAPTER ONE: Owlet Alarm!   119

CHAPTER TWO: The Most Enormous Yawn   129

CHAPTER THREE: Rock-a-bye Chameleon   139

CHAPTER FOUR: The Egg Hunt   147

CHAPTER FIVE: Jilly   157

CHAPTER ONE

Owlet Alarm!

"Delicious!" said Lily, wiping crumbs from her mouth with a napkin.

She and Jess sat with Bertie and Goldie at a long table in the Bake-Off hall. Between them, they had just polished off a big blossom pie with plenty of whipped cream, some raspberry eclairs and a thick

wedge of apple cake each.

"Best lunch ever!" said Bertie, his dark eyes shining.

Jess giggled and wiped a splodge of raspberry jam off the lion cub's whiskers. "Agreed! But we need to get going now, or we'll never find that third chameleon egg."

Lily and Jess had already found two of the eggs, with help from their friends Goldie and Bertie, but there was still one egg left to find. They couldn't let Grizelda win.

"Let's take a look at the list Mrs

Kinderbeak gave us," said Goldie. "We can see which families are still waiting for eggs to hatch."

Lily pulled it out of her pocket. "Only one family!" she said. "The Cleverfeathers are expecting a little owl chick!"

"Oh, that's wonderful news!" said Jess. Then her face fell. "But if they're the only family left on the list, it must be their egg that Grizelda has swapped for a chameleon egg!"

"Uh-oh …" muttered Goldie. "We'd better find them right away."

They hurried out of the hall, and at

once they saw Mr

Cleverfeather,

dressed in his

favourite

waistcoat

and monocle.

Their old owl friend was busy setting up

a stall in the middle of the meadow, with

Mr and Mrs Bigroar helping. The sign for

the stall said *Lucky Dip*.

"Goodness!" said Mr Cleverfeather.

"If it isn't young Liss and Jelly! I've just

been making friends with this mair

of parvellous lions! I mean, pair of

marvellous lions!"

Jess and Lily saw that other animals
were setting up stalls nearby, happily
chattering to each other. They didn't look
at all scared of the Bigroars any more.

"Have you come for the Funshine
Sete?" asked Mr Cleverfeather. "That is to
say, the Sunshine Fete! I've been making
some golly james for everyone to play!
There's a Dook a Huck, and Ness the
Gumber of Jeets in the Swar!"

"Er …" said Bertie, looking confused.

"He means Hook a Duck," whispered
Lily, smiling. "And Guess the Number of

Sweets in the Jar!"

"Oh, those sound really fun!" said
Bertie.

"Thank you, young cub!" said Mr
Cleverfeather. "And Mrs Cleverfeather
has been helping too. She's made some
nice blothes and clankets for the raffle. Of
course, she's not here yet. She's back at
my inventing shed, waiting for our darling
chittle lick to hatch!"

"Little chick, you mean!" said Lily. "But
that's why we're here, Mr Cleverfeather.
We're afraid that wicked witch Grizelda
has swapped your lovely egg for a

chameleon egg. She's already done it with two other eggs. And if the chameleon hatches, it'll cause all sorts of trouble!"

"By my feak and beathers!" gasped Mr Cleverfeather. "That's terrible! Whatever shall we—"

BLEEP BLEEP BLEEP! The owl was interrupted by a large brass watch strapped to his leg. Coloured lights flashed all across its face as it bleeped furiously.

"That's my Owlet Alarm!" cried Mr Cleverfeather, switching off the noise. "I made it myself. It means the egg is hatching night row!"

Mr Cleverfeather
led the way,
half running, half
fluttering through
the forest until they
reached the tree where
his inventing shed was
built.

As they approached,
the tree trunk began
to twist and whir.
Little wooden steps
appeared all around

it, clicking and clacking into place until a spiral staircase ran all the way to the top. The friends climbed up into the branches, where a rickety little wooden shed was perched.

Lily swung open the door, and there was Mrs Cleverfeather the snowy owl, peering down into a wooden cot in the middle of the room. Inside the cot, a cream-coloured egg rested on a puffy white cushion. A crack was already spreading across its shell. Then the egg burst open – *CRACK!* – and a shower of green sparks fell on the floor.

"Oh no …" gasped Jess. "I think we're too late!"

A glowing little green chameleon climbed out of the eggshell, yawned and snuggled down in the cot.

Mrs Cleverfeather jumped back in fright.

"You were right!" wailed Mr Cleverfeather. "Grizelda has nidkapped our egg!"

CHAPTER TWO

The Most Enormous Yawn

The chameleon curled up on the cushion, yawning again. Mrs Cleverfeather flapped desperately at it. "My baby!" she squawked. "Where's my baby?"

The little green lizard tried to hide under the blankets but Mrs Cleverfeather

pulled them back. The chameleon
scurried on to the edge of the cot and
leaped on to a table. At once the table
turned invisible, as though the chameleon
were running on thin air. He jumped
again, landing on an armchair which
vanished at once. Then he hopped down
on to the floor.

Jess and Lily blinked in disbelief as the
branches of the tree appeared all around
them.

"He's made the entire shed invisible!"
gasped Lily.

"I don't like this," muttered Jess, looking

down at her feet. "It's like we're floating in mid-air!"

"And if we can't see anything, we'll just keep bumping into things!" said Goldie anxiously.

"I'll get him!" cried Bertie. The little lion pounced, but the chameleon was too fast for him. He shot straight through an invisible window and went racing down the trunk, all the way to the ground, where he dashed off into the bushes.

"There, there, Mrs Cleverfeather," said Mr Cleverfeather, wrapping his wife up in his feathery wings. She was snuffling into

a handkerchief.

"We'll find your egg," said Jess.

"That's right – we promise," said Lily.

"And I'm going to help!" Bertie piped up. "My family are here to protect the forest, after all!"

Mrs Cleverfeather blew her beak in the handkerchief. "Oh, please bind my faby."

"Don't worry, we will," said Goldie. She led the way down from the tree, but even

the wooden steps had turned invisible, and
Jess and Lily had to cling on to the trunk
so that they didn't fall.

"I can't see anything suspicious," said
Jess, when they reached the ground.

Lily frowned. "I'm sure there were more
trees in the forest before … Oof!" She
bumped into something and staggered
away.

"It's an invisible tree!" said Bertie. "We'd
better go carefully!"

The friends set out through the forest,
creeping cautiously. But almost at once,
Goldie went head over heels. "Something

133

tripped me!" she said, rubbing at her elbow.

Just then, Lucy Longwhiskers the rabbit came hopping out from the trees up ahead. "Hello, girls!" she cried. "Is it me, or is something different about the forest today?"

"Look out!" called Jess.

THUMP! Lucy hopped straight into something invisible and went tumbling over. "Ouch!" she said,

sitting up and holding her nose. "That felt like a tree!"

"There's a naughty chameleon turning everything invisible," Lily explained. "Can you tell all the animals to be very careful, and stick to the paths?"

The sound of shouting and crashing floated through the air. The girls, Goldie and Bertie ran towards it.

"We're heading back towards Sunshine Meadow!" panted Goldie.

Sure enough, they came running out at the edge of the sunny field.

Animals were scurrying in all directions,

looking terribly anxious and wailing.

"The stalls have vanished!" cried Bertie.

They saw Mr Silverback stumble into something invisible and fall over. Then Mr Longwhiskers tripped on something else and went head-first into the pool of water for Hook a Duck, with a huge splash.

Jess ran over to Sarah Scramblepaw, who was sitting on the grass in floods of tears. "Are you all right, Sarah?" she asked, putting

her arm around the fluffy white fox cub.

"It's the chameleon!" sobbed Sarah. "He jumped on my big pile of cuddly toys, and they disappeared! They were going to be prizes for Hook a Duck."

"He jumped in our jar of marshmallows too!" cried Olivia Nibblesqueak.

"And in our basket of wool," added Mr Woollyhop.

"I think I know what this chameleon wants …" said Lily thoughtfully. "Remember how he tried to snuggle up in the cot? All these things are soft and

cuddly too. And, when he hatched, he gave the most enormous yawn!"

"He must be sleepy!" Goldie exclaimed.

"So that's how we can stop the spell," cried Jess. "Find a way to get the chameleon to sleep!"

CHAPTER THREE

Rock-a-bye Chameleon

"Blothes and clankets!" said Jess.

Everyone looked at her in puzzlement.

"Clothes and blankets," she said. "That's

what Mrs Cleverfeather made for the

raffle. We can use them to make a lovely

soft bed for the chameleon!"

"I see them!" said Bertie, and he shot

off to a big pile of thick, fleecy red
blankets right next to the *Lucky Dip*
banner. Gathering up an armful, he
hurried back. The girls took the blankets
to a pair of big trees at the edge of the
forest, right next to the meadow, where
it was quiet and shady. Then they got to
work, tying the blankets together to make
a big, soft red hammock. They hung it up
between the trees.

"Don't forget one to go on top!" said
Bertie, draping a third blanket over the
hammock. "That'll make it extra snuggly.
Now all we need is a pillow …"

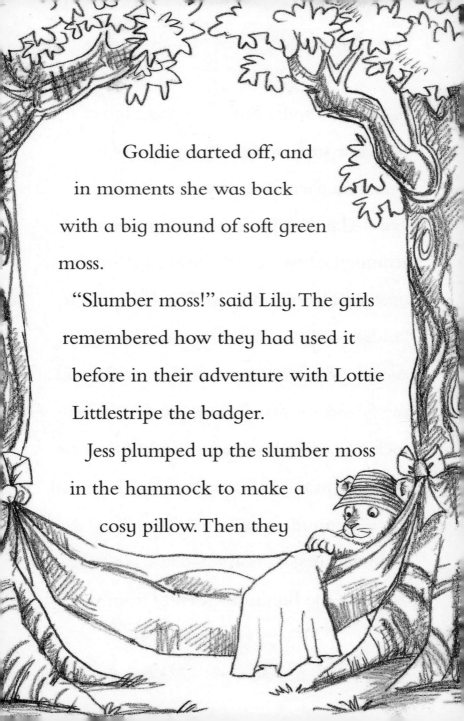

Goldie darted off, and
in moments she was back
with a big mound of soft green
moss.

"Slumber moss!" said Lily. The girls
remembered how they had used it
before in their adventure with Lottie
Littlestripe the badger.

Jess plumped up the slumber moss
in the hammock to make a
cosy pillow. Then they

hid behind some bushes at the edge of the meadow and waited …

At last, there was a rustling in the grass. The glowing green chameleon scampered towards the hammock, ran up a tree trunk and dived in. *Flumph!* He landed softly and the hammock swayed. At once the blankets turned invisible, and the friends could all see the chameleon rocking gently from side to side. He gave another huge yawn and squirmed around, getting comfortable.

Bertie crept out on tip-paws. He began to swing the hammock gently from side to side. Then he sang a lullaby.

"Rock-a-bye lizard, in the treetop ..."

His voice was so soft and calm that
even Jess and Lily began to feel sleepy.
They joined in, together with Goldie,
singing the lullaby over and over again.

Then, with a sudden *POP*, the
hammock came back into view, and all
they could see of the little chameleon
was his head, poking out from under the
blanket on top. His eyes were shut tight,
and he had begun to snore. The green
glow had faded.

"He's asleep!"

whispered Jess to her friends.

"And everything's turned visible again!"
added Lily. "Well done, Bertie. You might
not have a big scary roar, but your lovely
voice is just as useful!"

Bertie grinned. "I suppose you're right!"

Mrs Kinderbeak trundled over, gently
pushing her pram with the two
other sleeping chameleons.

The stork bent

low over the

hammock

and swept

up the third

chameleon, before carefully lowering him
into the pram with the others.

"It's most peculiar," said Mrs
Kinderbeak. "I've never seen any other
chameleons in the forest before … and
they weren't on my list! I wonder where
their parents are?"

"Maybe we can find them," said Jess.
"But first we've got to track down the
Cleverfeathers' egg."

"And we'd better hurry," said Lily.
"If we don't find it soon, the poor little
owl chick will hatch out without its
mummy and daddy!"

Jess pointed over to a little stage set up among the stalls. Mr Silverback the badger was standing there, announcing events with his shiny red megaphone.

"I have an idea," she said.

CHAPTER FOUR

The Egg Hunt

The girls ran over to the stage. "Hello, Mr Silverback," said Jess. "Would you mind if we made another quick announcement?"

"Of course not!" said the badger.

The girls scrambled on to the stage and took the megaphone. Jess lifted it up and pressed a button on the handle. "Hello,

 147

everyone!" she said, and her voice crackled out, magically carrying across the whole of Friendship Forest. "We've got a special game for you all to play now … the Egg Hunt!"

The animals in the meadow stopped what they were doing and turned to look at the girls. Jess passed the megaphone over to Lily. "Grizelda has stolen the poor

Cleverfeathers' egg," said Lily. "We have to find it before it hatches, or it'll be so frightened! Will you help us?"

There was a chorus of agreement from the animals and everyone got to work, hunting through the long grasses, under stalls and inside sacks of toys.

"Thank you, Mr Silverback," said Jess, handing back the megaphone.

Bertie and Goldie and the girls joined in the hunt. Lily rooted through the prizes for the tombola, while Jess dipped into the Hook a Duck paddling pool. Bertie dived into the barrel at the Lucky Dip, while Goldie sifted through popcorn at a little kiosk run by the Prickleback hedgehogs. But there was no sign of an egg anywhere.

"Hey!" said Lily, suddenly. "I think I see something funny at the coconut shy!"

The girls rushed over. Five posts were set up there, each with a coconut balanced on top. The coconuts were all big, brown and hairy ... except one. The last one was small and white.

Jess ran over and laid a hand on the object. "The Cleverfeathers' egg!" she cried. "We've found it!"

Lily went to join her and together, the girls carefully lifted the egg. But it was so smooth that it slipped. Down it went, toppling through their fingers.

"No!" cried both girls at once.

The egg tumbled, end over end ...

Then a flash of gold shot into the coconut shy. Mr Bigroar dived and – *thump!* The egg landed in his big, soft paw.

"You saved it!" cried Jess.

"Hooray for Mr Bigroar!" said Goldie.

The girls turned to see that Goldie and Bertie were there at the end of the shy, with all the other animals gathered round, smiling at Mr Bigroar. Everyone began to cheer.

WHHOOOSHH!

A glowing green orb zipped out of the sky towards them. It burst apart with a shower of smelly green sparks, and Grizelda appeared. She was scowling furiously, her crinkly green hair flying all around her.

"You meddling pests!" she screeched. "You've foiled my plans for the very last time … Now I'm going to destroy that precious egg of yours!" Grizelda thrust her hand at Mr Bigroar, and green light crackled around her fingers.

"She's going to cast a spell!" gasped Lily. She and Jess dived forward, hugging on tight to Mr Bigroar and shielding the egg with their bodies.

"GRRRRAAOOORRR!"

The girls flinched and covered their ears. The roar had come from the far end of the coconut shy, so loud that it blew everyone's hair back and ruffled Grizelda's cloak.

The witch shrieked with fear. "Nooooo!" she shrieked, clamping her hands over her ears. "Make it stop!" The green light flickered into nothing.

"Was that noise … Bertie?" gasped Jess.

"He's found his roar!" said Lily.

The little lion club stood proudly in front of all the animals, his fur bristling. He glared at Grizelda and opened his jaws one more time.

"GRRRRAAAOOOOOOORR!!"

Grizelda shrieked again, even louder.
She stumbled backwards, caught her high
heel on a tree root and sprawled on the
ground. Bertie took a pace towards her.

"Please don't hurt me!" Grizelda cried.
She was quivering all over.

"I'll let you go," said Bertie, "but only if
you promise to stay away from Friendship
Forest for ever."

Grizelda's face twisted into a scowl.
"For ever?" she said. "But I've got to come
back to take over the forest—"

"GRRRRAAAOOOOOOORR!!"

155

roared Bertie again.

"All right!" Grizelda shrieked. "I promise I won't come back. I'll never hurt the animals again – just please don't eat me!" Then she ran away across the meadow with her cloak and hair streaming behind her.

The girls laughed. They knew that lovely Bertie would never hurt anyone. But he'd got rid of Grizelda with his massive roar.

"You did it, Bertie!" the girls cried.

CHAPTER FIVE

Jilly

The animals of Friendship Forest cheered
and gathered round the Bigroars.

"You lions are some of the bravest,
nicest creatures we've ever met!" cried Mr
Silverback. "We're so pleased you came to
Friendship Forest!"

Just then, a chameleon ran into the

meadow. She was much bigger than the babies, with a curly tail and a pair of red sunglasses perched on her forehead. Her skin flickered blue and silver, and she was frowning anxiously.

"Excuse me," said the chameleon. "I am Mrs Rainbowtail, and I'm looking for some eggs. A witch stole three from our home on Sunbeam Island. I don't suppose any of you have seen them?"

"Yes, we have," said Jess. "Where's Mrs Kinderbeak?"

The animals made way and Mrs Kinderbeak came through, wheeling her pram. The three chameleon babies had woken up now and were playing happily, chasing each other's tails.

"My babies! They've hatched!" cried Mrs Rainbowtail. "Spangle, Opal and Prism!" She swept them up, all the colours of the rainbow flashing across her skin.

The baby chameleons copied their mother, until all four of them were shimmering with beautiful colours.

The girls explained what had happened. Mrs Rainbowtail thanked

them for finding her babies and lifting the enchantment.

"They're beautiful," said Goldie, gently stroking one of the chameleons. "And so much happier now they've got their mummy back!"

Captain Ace the stork stepped forward, standing smartly to attention. "Pardon me, ma'am, but perhaps I might offer you some assistance? I'll have you back on Sunbeam Island in no time, if you'll just hop into my hot air balloon?"

"Oh, yes please!" said Mrs Rainbowtail. The girls and their friends waved to

the Rainbowtails as Captain Ace's hot
air balloon rose up into the sky, and flew
towards Sunbeam Island.

"Now to get this egg to the
Cleverfeathers!" said Jess.

Back in the inventing shed, the girls,
Bertie, Goldie and the Cleverfeathers
were all gathered around the cot.

A crack spread across the shell.

Everyone held their breath. A little
bit of shell fell off … then another, and
finally the whole top of the egg cracked
and dropped on to the cushion. Inside

the egg crouched a tiny, feathered little
creature, speckled white and brown.
She looked up with huge dark eyes and
blinked.

"What a beautiful little owlet!"
breathed Jess.

Mr Cleverfeather reached in with
his wing and scooped up his chick. He
rocked her gently, then passed her to Mrs
Cleverfeather.

"She's wonderful!" cooed Mrs
Cleverfeather.

"How can we ever thank you?" said
Mr Cleverfeather to the girls. "You saved

our little owlet.

Thank you,

Goldie. Thank

you, Bertie, and

thank you Less

and Jilly! I mean,

Liss and Jelly! I mean … er … Jilly?"

Jess and Lily giggled.

"That's it!" said Mrs Cleverfeather

suddenly. Everyone turned to look at her.

"Jilly is the perfect name for our little

chick. Little Jilly Cleverfeather!"

The girls looked at each other and

grinned. "An owlet named after us," said

Lily. "I can't believe it!"

"Tweet!" said Jilly, and everyone laughed and crowded round to stroke her soft little head.

Back at the Midsummer Festival, the big concert had just begun. The girls sat on a blanket on the grass and watched the Friendship Forest Secret Singers all troop on to the stage, led by Grace Woollyhop the lamb.

"We have a special surprise for you," said Grace, through Mr Silverback's shiny red megaphone. "So many beautiful little babies have been born today, we thought we'd sing them some lullabies. And we're going to use this megaphone, so all the little ones tucked up in their cots can hear it, all through the forest. All together now…"

The Secret Singers gathered round the megaphone and sang into it.

"Sparkle, sparkle, little sparkleberries…"

The girls joined in, and so did the animals, until the whole meadow was singing along. But the loudest by far were Mr and Mrs Bigroar the lions, and their little cub Bertie.

"He doesn't need a megaphone!"
laughed Jess. "I'm so glad he found his
voice!"

Next the Secret Singers sang *She'll
Be Coming Round Spelltop Mountain*, and
finally *Here We Go Round the Friendship
Tree*. As the sun began to set, Jess and Lily
knew it was time to go home.

"Goodbye, Bertie," said Jess, going over
to hug the lion cub.

Lily hugged him too. "We'll miss you!
You're the best big brother we've ever
met, and we know you're going to keep
Friendship Forest safe from that wicked

Grizelda!"

"Goodbye,
girls," said
Bertie, his tail
swishing with
happiness.

"Come back soon!"

"We promise," said Jess and Lily.

Then Goldie led the girls away through
the twilit forest, all the way to the
Friendship Tree.

"That was an amazing day," sighed
Jess. "We saw so many babies being born!
And thank goodness the Bigroars are here

now to keep Friendship Forest safe."

"Yes … perhaps you won't even need our help any more," said Lily, feeling sad at the thought.

"But we'll always need friends," said Goldie firmly, her big green eyes twinkling as she gave them each a big hug.

Then together, the girls swung open the door in the Friendship Tree and stepped into the golden light …

"Here, girl!" called Jess. "Here, boy!"

Back in the garden at Helping Paw, the puppies were nowhere to be seen. But

as soon as Lily brought out a paper bag
of dog treats, two golden bolts came
shooting out from their hiding places
under the hedge.

Lily tossed a treat to one little chow-
chow, who caught it in her mouth. "Sit!"
she told the other puppy.

The chow-chow sat and barked —
except it was such a little bark, it was
more of a squeak.

Lily grinned as she fed him his treat.
"Does that remind you of anyone?"

Jess bent down to stroke the puppy.
"Don't worry, little one," she told him.

"You'll find your bark one day … just like Bertie found his roar!"

The girls smiled at each other, thinking of Bertie and all their other friends. They were safe and sound in the magical world of Friendship Forest, just as Lily and Jess were safe at home. After all this time, the wicked witch Grizelda was no more, but the friendships they'd made in the forest would last for ever.

The End

Join Lily and Jess on their very first adventure in Friendship Forest!

Find out how it all began in

Lucy Longwhiskers
Gets Lost

Lily Hart stepped into the long garden, breathing in the scent of the dewy grass. In the distance, nestled behind a copse of trees, was the barn her parents had turned into the Helping Paw Wildlife Hospital. Lily shrugged a sleeveless cardigan over her stripy green dress, then picked up the bucket of lettuce leaves waiting by the back door. Swinging it over her arm, she walked over to a large run with a wire fence. At the end of the run was a wooden hutch.

"Breakfast time!" Lily called. A pink, whiskery nose poked out from one of the hutch's doors, then another. Soon three rabbits were hopping towards Lily. Two of them had bandages on their paws and the other had a bandage over its ear.

Lily opened the top of the run and tipped the lettuce leaves into a bowl.

"Eat up," she murmured. Her bobbed dark hair had fallen across her face and Lily tucked it behind an ear as she watched the rabbits nibble the leaves. *They're nearly better now*, she thought. *They'll soon be ready to go back to their burrow.*

A flash of movement from the row of

houses across the lane caught Lily's eye. One of the front doors had opened, and out came a blonde girl in denim shorts, leggings and a pink hoodie.

Lily smiled. It was Jess Forester – her best friend!

Jess checked that the lane was clear and hurried to the garden gate. She grinned as Lily ran to meet her.

Read

Lucy Longwhiskers Gets Lost

to find out what happens next!

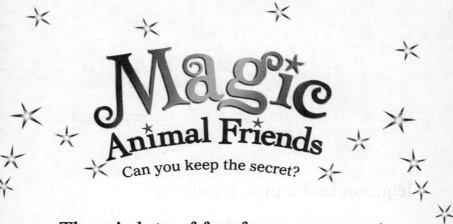

Can you keep the secret?

There's lots of fun for everyone at
www.magicanimalfriends.com

Play games and explore the secret world of
Friendship Forest, where animals can talk!

Join the
Magic Animal Friends Club!

✶ Special competitions ✶

✶ Exclusive content ✶

✶ All the latest Magic Animal Friends news! ✶

To join the Club, simply go to

www.magicanimalfriends.com/join-our-club/

If you like
Magic Animal Friends,
you'll love…

Welcome to Animal Ark!

Animal-mad Amelia is sad
about moving house, until she discovers
Animal Ark, where vets look after all
kinds of animals in need.

Join Amelia and her friend Sam for a
brand-new series of animal adventures!